The Tempest

Based on the play by
William Shakespeare

Retold by Rosie Dickins
Illustrated by Christa Unzner

Reading consultant: Alison Kelly
Roehampton University

❋ About the story ❋

This story is based on a famous play by William Shakespeare, written about 400 years ago. It's set on a lonely island, with the following characters...

Prospero, magician and ex-Duke of Milan. Thrown out of Milan by his brother, ending up on the island.

Ariel, Prospero's fairy servant. Can make himself invisible.

Caliban, Prospero's servant. Very grumpy.

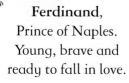

Ferdinand, Prince of Naples. Young, brave and ready to fall in love.

Miranda, Prospero's daughter. Grows up on the island, remembering nothing of her past.

Alonso, King of Naples and Ferdinand's father. Helped to plot against Prospero.

Gonzalo, a kind old lord. When Prospero was attacked by his brother, Gonzalo helped him escape.

Sebastian, King Alonso's brother. Envies Alonso's crown.

Antonio, Prospero's brother. Attacked Prospero and made himself false Duke of Milan.

Trinculo, the King's jester. Always making jokes.

Stephano, the King's butler. Kind but vain.

As the play begins, Ferdinand, King Alonso and their followers are on a ship in a storm – a magical storm, called up by Prospero to bring them to the island.

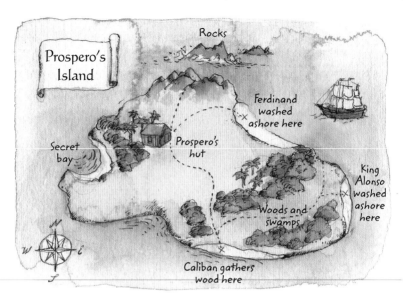

Prospero's Island

Rocks

Ferdinand
washed
ashore here

Secret
bay

Prospero's
hut

King
Alonso
washed
ashore
here

Woods and
swamps

N
W · E
S

Caliban gathers
wood here

When you see lines written like this, it means
they are Shakespeare's original words.

✻ Contents ✻

❈ Chapter 1 ❈

The storm

Miranda stood on the island, gazing out to sea – where a wild storm was raging. The wind whipped the waves into a frenzy. In the distance, she heard desperate shouts. A ship was being driven onto the rocks...

She ran to find her father, Prospero
the magician. "Please calm the
storm," she begged. "There's a ship
with people on it out there!"

"They won't be hurt," promised
Prospero, lowering his magic staff.
He looked at Miranda. "I called up
the storm for you. If you only knew..."

"Knew what?" asked Miranda.

"You are too young to remember, but I was once a Prince, and the Duke of Milan. And you were a Princess."

"Oh!" gasped Miranda. "Then how did we come to this island?"

7

"My brother, Antonio, made a plot with King Alonso of Naples," explained Prospero. "With the King's help, Antonio stole my dukedom and tried to drown us. Luckily, my old friend Gonzalo helped us to escape in a boat. After many days at sea, we drifted here."

"But why did you create the storm?" asked Miranda.

"To bring my old enemies here, and mend our fortunes," said Prospero. "But enough talk!"

He didn't want Miranda to know everything just yet. He waved his hand and her eyes closed.

Prospero gripped his staff and called his fairy servant. "Ariel!"
"Hail, master!" sang the fairy.
"Have you done all I asked?" said Prospero.

"Yes," answered Ariel.
"The castaways are safe and
spread out around the island.
The King and his followers are
in one part, his servants are in
another, and Prince Ferdinand is
alone on the shore."

11

"And the ship?" asked Prospero.

"It's moored in a secret bay, with the sailors asleep on board."

"Good," said Prospero. "Soon I will set you free. But first, I have just a few more tasks for you."

❋ Chapter 2 ❋

Love at first sight

Strange music played around Prince Ferdinand's ears. It was Ariel, singing. But the fairy had made himself invisible, so the sound seemed to come out of nowhere.

"It must be magic," thought Ferdinand, listening closely.

Full fathom five thy father lies;
Of his bones are coral made;
Those are pearls that were his eyes...

"Alas," groaned Ferdinand. "The singer says my father is drowned."

Lost in his sadness, he didn't notice Prospero approaching with Miranda.

"What do you see?" Prospero asked his daughter.

"Someone very handsome," sighed Miranda. "Is he a kind of fairy?"

Prospero laughed. "No, he's a man. He was cast ashore by the storm."

At the sound of their voices,
Ferdinand looked up. When he saw
Miranda, his heart leaped. He had
never seen anyone so lovely.

"Are you a goddess?" he said in
wonder.

It was Miranda's turn to laugh.
"No, I'm just a girl. Who are *you*?"

"Ferdinand, Prince of Naples," he
answered boldly. "Or rather, *King*
– for I fear my father is drowned…"
He blushed, then blurted out, "And
if you would have me, I would
willingly make you my Queen."

Miranda clapped her hands
in delight.

Prospero nodded to himself. His plans were working – his daughter and the King's son had fallen in love at first sight. "But I mustn't make it too easy for them," he told himself. "I must test their love."

"Enough!" he said sternly. "This man is a spy. He wants to steal my island."

"No!" cried Miranda.

There's nothing ill can dwell in such a temple.

Prospero ignored her. "I will put the villain in chains and make him carry logs," he said, raising his staff. "Follow me!" And by magic, he forced Ferdinand to obey.

19

Miranda watched sadly as
Ferdinand tramped to and fro,
laden with heavy logs.

"Don't work so hard," she
whispered, as soon as Prospero was
out of sight. "Let me carry your
logs while you rest."

"No, my lady," replied Ferdinand gallantly. "I'd rather die than watch you do my work. And I don't suffer, so long as you are near."

Admired Miranda...
The very instant that I saw you,
My heart did fly to your service...

Miranda's eyes shone. "You are mine, and I am yours," she promised.

✱ Chapter 3 ✱

More castaways

Meanwhile, on the far side of the island, King Alonso was worrying about his son.

"I fear Ferdinand is drowned," he moaned.

Lord Gonzalo tried to comfort him.

"I saw the Prince swimming," said Gonzalo. "He may have come ashore."

The King shook his head sadly.

Two younger Lords watched him, smirking. They were Antonio, brother of Prospero, and Sebastian, brother of the King.

"What a fuss," sneered Antonio.

He receives comfort like cold porridge.

Just then, a strange music started up. Ariel, invisible to the castaways, was casting a spell. In moments, King Alonso and Lord Gonzalo were fast asleep.

"How odd," remarked Sebastian. "I don't feel sleepy at all."

"No, nor me," agreed Antonio.
"But seeing those two lying there
gives me an idea." He paused
slyly, then went on. "With Prince
Ferdinand gone, you are the
King's heir. If anything
should happen to him..."

Sebastian grinned eagerly. "Like what happened to Prospero, when you took the dukedom?"

Antonio nodded. "Quick, let's strike now!" Together, he and Sebastian drew their swords...

Hastily, Ariel woke the sleepers.

If of life you keep a care, Shake off slumber and beware. Awake, awake!

"Aargh," yelled Gonzalo.

"Why the swords?" cried the King.

"We were just trying, er, to protect you," lied Sebastian. "We heard a bellowing. It must have been lions..."

"A *lot* of lions," agreed Antonio. "Didn't you hear them?"

27

"Some kind of noise woke me," admitted Gonzalo. "We'd better be careful from now on."

"Let's go and search for my son," broke in the King, refreshed by his sleep. "If Gonzalo is right, he may be somewhere on this island."

Ariel watched the four men go, then flew off to tell Prospero what he had done.

Chapter 4

Magic and mayhem

Down on the beach, a huge, scowling man was picking up driftwood. It was Caliban, another servant of Prospero's, gathering fuel for their fire.

"I wish Prospero had never come to this island," he muttered.

"I was King here till *he* came," Caliban went on. "Now I have to do what he says, or he sends fairies to pinch me." He heard footsteps. "Uh-oh, here comes one of them now." He dropped flat on his face and covered himself with his cloak.

But Caliban was wrong. It was not a fairy, but a castaway from the ship – Trinculo, the King's jester.

"What's this – man or fish?" said Trinculo, spotting the cloak. He lifted a corner, wrinkling his nose in disgust. "It *smells* like a fish."

A very ancient and fish-like smell...

"Aha! I see arms and legs. Maybe
it's an islander who was struck by
lightning. Now it's starting to rain.
I'd better take shelter." And Trinculo
crawled under the cloak too.

32

No sooner had Trinculo vanished from sight than another castaway arrived – Stephano, the King's butler. He was carrying a bottle and singing merrily.

He stopped short when he saw the cloak. "What's this? A monster with four legs!"

Caliban thought the newcomer was a fairy. "Please don't hurt me," he begged, shuddering under the cloak.

"It's got the shakes," exclaimed Stephano. "Here, this'll cure you." He put his bottle in Caliban's hand.

34

"That sounds like Stephano," muttered Trinculo, beneath the cloak.

"Four legs and two voices – it's definitely a monster!" cried Stephano.

"No, no – it's me!" said Trinculo, throwing off the cloak.

Caliban took a swig from the bottle and smiled deeply. "That tastes heavenly," he sighed. "I'll worship the man who gave it to me." And he kissed Stephano's feet.

"Well, since the King and Prince are drowned, I may as well rule here," laughed Stephano, taking back his bottle. "Monster, show us your island!"

So Caliban led the two castaways around the island – all the while complaining about Prospero. The grumpy servant had no idea that an invisible Ariel was listening to his every word.

"Prospero stole my island by magic," Caliban told Stephano. "I wish you ruled here instead. You could take his place, if you knocked him on the head..."

"Monster, I will," promised Stephano airily.

"I'd better stop this," thought Ariel. He began to hum, to lead the would-be killers astray.

"What's that?" cried Stephano and Trinculo, startled.

"Come, let's follow the sound," called Caliban, bewitched.

The isle is full of noises,
Sounds and sweet airs,
that give delight and hurt not.

❋ Chapter 5 ❋

Old enemies and young lovers

The King and his followers were tired and hungry, and losing heart with their search for Ferdinand.

"We've looked everywhere," sighed the King. "He must have drowned."

"Lucky for you," Antonio hissed to Sebastian. Sebastian grinned.

Unseen by them, Prospero had
been watching his old enemies.
Now, he cast a spell.

The four castaways watched,
open-mouthed, as a table laden
with food appeared out of nowhere.
Hungrily, they ran over to it
– and, with a clap of thunder, it
disappeared again.

A fierce voice rang out. "Wicked men! Remember how you stole Prospero's dukedom, and left him and his daughter to drown. Now the sea has taken your loved ones, and you are castaways here. This is your punishment."

Sebastian and Antonio reached
for their swords, but found they
could not lift the blades. The King
just stood, wild-eyed with grief.

"Their guilt is written on their
faces," thought Gonzalo, watching.

At the same time as his father was weeping, Ferdinand was happier than he had thought possible. Prospero had suddenly reappeared, released the Prince and given him permission to marry Miranda!

"I had to test your love," Prospero explained. "You passed the test and won my daughter. So be glad."

Ferdinand clasped Miranda's hands in joy, while Prospero called Ariel.

"Bring us a show to celebrate the occasion," he whispered to the fairy.

Ariel nodded and began to hum, conjuring up a vision of three goddesses. Ferdinand and Miranda watched, delighted, as the goddesses sang of rich harvests and happy marriages. Then they blessed the happy couple, before melting back into the air.

Hourly joys be still upon you!
Let us sing our blessings on you.

"This is paradise," sighed
Ferdinand happily.

"But I nearly forgot," muttered Prospero, frowning. "There is still Caliban's plot to worry about... He and his friends would have me gone like this vision!" Suddenly, the magician looked old and tired.

"Are you all right, Father?"
exclaimed Miranda.

"I must take a walk," insisted
Prospero. "Ariel, come with me."

49

Making themselves invisible,
Prospero and Ariel went to find
the plotters – who were wading
through a marsh and squabbling.

"We should never have followed that music," groaned Stephano. "Now I've dropped my bottle!"

"Hush," hissed Caliban. "We're nearly at Prospero's hut."

Stephano gave a drunken grin.

Ariel hummed a spell, and a
string of fresh, gleaming clothes
appeared on the trees. Trinculo and
Stephano rushed over and began
trying them on.

"No, no," moaned Caliban.
"You're wasting time..."

Ariel hummed a little louder, and suddenly the air filled with the cries of hunting dogs. The three plotters dropped everything and fled.

"Now all my enemies are at my mercy," said Prospero. "My work is nearly done."

"Your spells have filled Alonso and Antonio with sadness and regret," Ariel told his master. "You'll feel sorry for them when you see them."

"I will not harm them," promised Prospero. "Bring them all to me."

Ariel nodded, and flew away.

Chapter 6

Happy ever after

Prospero looked around at the island where he had spent so many years. "I have commanded sun and wind and weather," he said. "But I will give up my magic. When this is done, I'll break my staff and drown my book of spells."

55

His thoughts were interrupted by Ariel, returning with the castaways and Caliban.

"Welcome friends," cried Prospero to the amazed gathering. "Behold, I am Prospero, rightful Duke of Milan."

King Alonso shook his head in confusion. "I don't know how this can be. But if you are Prospero, I beg your forgiveness."

"I forgive you *all*," said Prospero. "Even though I know some of you have been making plots!"

Caliban and Stephano trembled, and Antonio and Sebastian exchanged guilty looks.

"King, I share your loss," Prospero went on. "Today, in the storm, you lost a son and I lost a daughter."

"Oh heavens, if only they were alive, they could be King and Queen of Naples!" sighed King Alonso. "I'd gladly give my life for theirs."

Prospero smiled – and pulled back a curtain of ivy, to reveal Ferdinand and Miranda playing chess. Alonso gasped.

Miranda gazed back at the strange lords in amazement. She had never seen so many men.

Oh brave new world,
That has such people in it!

Ferdinand ran to embrace his father and introduce Miranda. "This lady is to be my wife," he said gaily.

"A happy ending," cried Gonzalo. "Ferdinand has found a wife, and Prospero has found his dukedom."

Prospero nodded wisely. "Look down at the bay," he said. "Your ship is ready to take us home. It only remains for me to free my servants. Caliban, the island is yours once more. Ariel, be free!"

Prospero watched as the whole party set off down to the bay, talking busily of what they would do when they got home.

When they were out of sight, he quietly put down his staff and book – and with them, his magic powers. He turned and spoke, as if asking an unseen audience for applause.

Now my charms are overthrown,
And what strength I have's my own...
Let me not... dwell
In this bare island by your spell;
But release me from my bands
With the help of your good hands.

Then, with a bow, he followed
the others down to the ship.

❋ William Shakespeare ❋
1564-1616

William Shakespeare was
born in Stratford-upon-Avon,
England, and became famous
as an actor and writer when he moved to
London. He wrote many poems and almost forty
plays which are still performed and enjoyed today.

❋ Usborne Quicklinks ❋

You can find out more about Shakespeare
by going to the Usborne Quicklinks Website
at **www.usborne-quicklinks.com** and
typing in the keywords 'yr tempest'.
Please follow the internet safety guidelines
on the Usborne Quicklinks Website.

Designed by Michelle Lawrence
Series designer: Russell Punter
Series editor: Lesley Sims
Digital manipulation: Nick Wakeford

First published in 2010 by Usborne Publishing Ltd., Usborne House,
83-85 Saffron Hill, London EC1N 8RT, England. www.usborne.com
Copyright © 2010 Usborne Publishing Ltd.